Marcus Pfister

Dazzle
the
Dinosaur

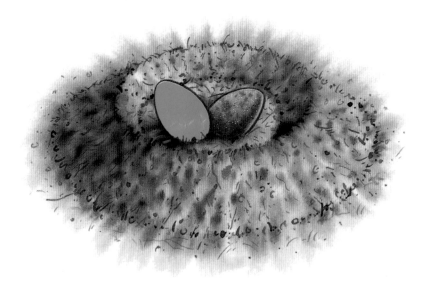

Nort...
New Yo...

One day Mother Maiasaurus found an extra egg in her nest.
"Where could this have come from?" she wondered as she
quickly covered up the eggs. The valley was not a safe place.
Food and water were hard to find. Dangerous dinosaurs lived
nearby. The eggs needed to be protected.

The other Maiasauruses were curious about this odd looking egg. As soon as the two eggs started to crack, they all came running to see what would hatch.

From Mother's own egg, out stepped a sweet-looking baby Maiasaurus girl. Then, **CRAAACK!** A little blue dinosaur with a row of sparkling scales popped out of the other egg.

"What kind of dinosaur are *you*?" everyone asked.

"I don't know," the little dinosaur said shyly.

"It doesn't matter," said Mother Maiasaurus. "We'll call you Dazzle."

Mother Maiasaurus named her little girl Maia.
Soon Maia and Dazzle were best friends. Every day
they went out to play. But they were never allowed
to go beyond the edge of the trees. The big world
was a dangerous place.

One night Maia and Dazzle were awake when they should have been asleep.

"Let's go exploring," said Dazzle.

"We can't," said Maia. "Our valley is too dangerous. What if we meet up with a Tyrannosaurus Rex?"

"We need a safer place to live," said Dazzle. "Come on, Maia. Maybe we can find one."

So Dazzle and Maia set off.

In the morning, the two little dinosaurs climbed up a pile of rocks.

"From way up here, we might see a good place to live," said Maia.

But just then, the rocks beneath them rumbled
and shook. Was it an earthquake?

Maia and Dazzle tumbled to the ground. A giant Stegosaurus stood in front of them. They hadn't been climbing rocks. They'd been climbing the Stegosaurus's back!

"You are lucky it was me you climbed on, and not a Tyrannosaurus Rex!" said the Stegosaurus. "What are you children doing way out here?"

"We're looking for a safe new home," said Dazzle.

"Well, be careful," said the kind Stegosaurus.

"We will!" said Maia, and they set off again, keeping a close eye out for danger.

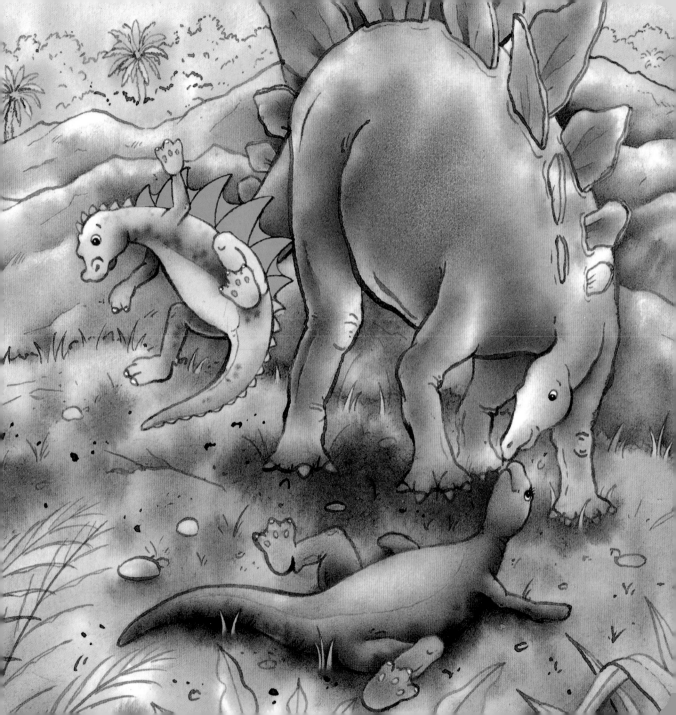

Suddenly they heard the thunder of giant footsteps.
Tyrannosaurus Rex!

"Run!" cried Maia. "Hide!"

Dazzle dashed under the branches and in and out of
shadows. But every time the sunlight flashed on his bright
scales, the T. Rex gave a mighty roar and plunged after him.

Dazzle dived into a patch of tall grass. He curled up and
hid his scales. Then he held his breath and waited.

T. Rex crashed through the bushes, looking for Dazzle. At last he gave up and stomped off.

"That was a close call!" said Maia.

"It sure was," Dazzle agreed.

The two little dinosaurs were worn out after their close call. So they found a nice warm tree trunk and curled up next to it. Then they fell fast asleep.

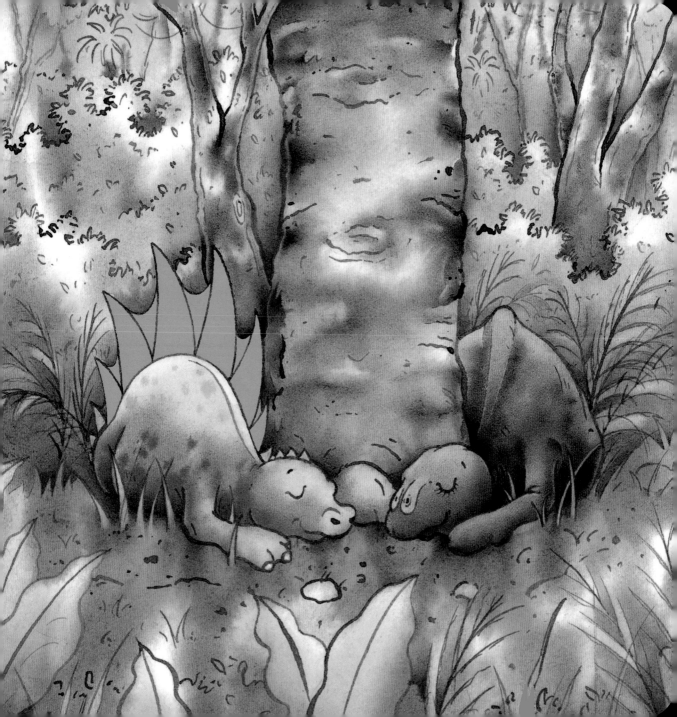

They didn't wake up until their tree trunk lifted
up from the ground and shook itself.
"Sorry to disturb you," said an Apatosaurus.
"But my leg was going to sleep. What are you
little ones doing out here, anyway?"
"We're looking for a safe home," said Dazzle.
"Our valley is too dangerous," said Maia.
"Maybe I can help," said the Apatosaurus.

The Apatosaurus lifted his head above the trees and called to a Quetzalcoatlus.

"I'll take you to the mountains," the Quetzalcoatlus agreed. "You may find a home there."

The Quetzalcoatlus dropped them on the mountainside. "Look around quickly," he told them. "You mustn't be out at night when the Dragonsaurus wakes up. I'll come back at sunset to take you home." Then he flew off.

"Look!" shouted Dazzle. "There's a cave!"

"A cave would be a very safe place to live," said Maia. "But who is that?" She crept inside to see.

Oh, no! The Dragonsaurus! Maia was trapped!

Dazzle thought fast. He turned his back so that his scales caught the sunlight. They glittered and glowed. Dazzle shone their light straight into the eyes of the Dragonsaurus.

The Dragonsaurus *hated* light. He ran out of the cave to escape. He never wanted to see that bright, shiny monster again!

"What did you do to the Dragonsaurus?" the
Quetzalcoatlus asked when he returned. "I saw him
running down the mountainside."

"Dazzle scared him off with his dazzling scales," said
Maia proudly.

The Quetzalcoatlus flew the two little dinosaurs back
to their family so they could tell everyone the great news.
The next day, they all moved into their new cave.

"Tomorrow we can explore the mountain," said Maia.

"All by ourselves," said Dazzle.

"Yes," Mother Maiasaurus agreed. "You will be safe here.
You have found a perfect home for your family."